D0118549

Scholastic Canada Ltd.
604 King Street West, Toronto, Ontario M5V 1E1, Canada
Scholastic Inc.
557 Broadway, New York, NY 10012, USA
Scholastic Australia Pty Limited
PO Box 579, Gosford, NSW 2250, Australia
Scholastic New Zealand Limited
Private Bag 94407, Botany, Manukau 2163, New Zealand
Scholastic Children's Books
Euston House, 24 Eversholt Street, London NW1 1DB, UK

Library and Archives Canada Cataloguing in Publication
Larry, H. I
Blockbuster / by H.I. Larry ; illustrations by Andy Hook.
(Zac Power)
ISBN 978-1-4431-1322-9
I. Hook, Andy II. Title. III. Series: Larry, H. I. Zac Power.
PZ7.L333Bl 2012   j823'.92   C2011-905478-7

Text copyright © 2007 by H.I. Larry
Illustration and design copyright © 2007 Hardie Grant Egmont
All rights reserved.
Published in Australia by Hardie Grant Egmont, 2007
First Canadian edition published, 2012.
Cover and illustrations by Andy Hook
Based on original illustration and design by Ash Oswald

6 5 4 3 2 1   Printed in Canada 116   11 12 13 14

ZAC POWER

[24 HOURS TO SAVE THE WORLD ... AND WRITE A THANK-YOU NOTE]

BLOCKBUSTER

BY *H. I. LARRY*

ILLUSTRATIONS BY *ANDY HOOK*

Scholastic Canada Ltd.

Toronto New York London Auckland Sydney
Mexico City New Delhi Hong Kong Buenos Aires

CHAPTER... ...ONE

It was 4:30 p.m. School was officially over for the day. So why was Zac Power still stuck in a classroom, pretending to look interested in fractions?

Stupid Homework Club, he huffed to himself. Kids whose parents worked late went to Homework Club and finished their homework while they waited to be picked up. But really, Zac didn't need any teacher watching him while his parents were working. After all, he was a top international spy who'd been on tons of missions by *himself*.

Zac's brother Leon and their parents were spies, too. They worked for the Government Investigation Bureau, or GIB for short. Zac's parents were taking an advanced code-breaking course. So Zac had to attend Homework Club all week, even though he was twelve years old.

Ms Tran, Zac's teacher, was supervising Homework Club that day. Zac heaved a gusty sigh and flicked open his math book. Ms Tran looked over at him and smiled.

Isn't learning math fun? her eyes seemed to twinkle.

Zac tried to keep his eyes open, but it was so hot in the classroom. The air stank of ripe bananas and other people's feet.

Suddenly, there was a knock at the door, and it swung open to a stern figure in a skirt and suit jacket. Mrs. De Souza, the school principal!

"Zachary Power," said Mrs. De Souza "Please step outside for a moment."

Zac sat bolt upright. Zachary? This must be serious. Only his parents called him Zachary, and even then, only when he was in big trouble.

The other kids stared as Zac leapt up.

Zac racked his brains for what he could have done. He'd missed a lot of school lately. He'd been so busy on important international missions! But he didn't think he was failing or anything.

"Well, Zac," said Mrs. De Souza, closing the classroom door. "I don't usually interrupt Homework Club, but the young girl who delivered this insisted that I give it to you right away."

Phew! He wasn't in trouble after all — but what was she giving him?

"What was her name again? It started with C…" said the principal, vaguely. "Never mind," she finished, handing Zac a glittering gold envelope.

Splashed across the front in curly black letters were the words:

For the urgent attention of
Mr. Zachary Power

His next mission from GIB? It had to be! Although it was weird that everyone was calling him Zachary all of a sudden...

Zac didn't think about it too long. A mission would get him out of Homework Club, and right now that was *all* that mattered.

Zac tore open the envelope. But it wasn't a new mission. It was something even better.

To thank you for accomplishing so many spy missions, GIB invites you to the premiere of a blockbuster movie:

COVERT OPERATIONS

Where: Nightshade Theatre, Hollywood
When: 5 p.m. tomorrow
Dress: Formal
Transportation: Provided

Awesome! Zac was getting out of school, and he didn't even have to stress over any difficult spy work. This time, things would be strictly Mission: Fun.

Zac looked at his watch. He had to get a move on if he wanted to get to Hollywood. The premiere was in 24 hours!

Mrs. De Souza talked about Homework Club, and Zac smiled politely. But he wasn't listening. Zac had noticed a strange sound — a kind of low hum unlike anything he'd heard before.

It was a bit like an engine, but it didn't growl like the fighter jet Zac had trained on. It wasn't an ordinary passenger plane either.

"I should probably get going," Zac said, waving the gold envelope at Mrs. De Souza. She nodded and stalked away.

Zac fished around in his pocket for his SpyPad, the mini-computer that all GIB spies carried. It had tons of cool functions, including a powerful mini-telescope. If there was some weird aircraft in the sky, Zac would easily be able to spot it.

Zac raced outside. He looked up, SpyPad at the ready. But Zac didn't need

a telescope to see what hovered in the sky above him.

It was an enormous, shiny gold blimp. Across the side, in giant black letters, were the words *Covert Operations*. This bling-covered blimp must be Zac's transportation to Hollywood!

How am I going to get up there, though? he wondered. But before he could blink, a red velvet rope swung down from the blimp's cabin.

Zac grabbed the rope. His feet lifted off the ground.

He was headed for Hollywood!

CHAPTER... ...TWO

It seemed slightly weird to Zac that GIB would send a flashy gold blimp to pick him up. Normally GIB was paranoid about being noticed.

But Zac didn't dwell on his doubts for too long. The blimp was even cooler inside than it looked from the outside!

The cabin was carpeted with white fluffy

rugs. There were mounds of chocolate bars in crystal bowls dotted around the cabin.

And, although the blimp could have carried lots of people, it looked like Zac was the only passenger.

A woman in a long, white apron appeared. Zac had never seen her before. *Strange,* he thought. He knew pretty much all the local GIB staff. *Maybe she's from the Hollywood office?*

"Please make yourself comfortable, Mr. Power," she said smoothly.

Zac's reclining seat was soft and wide. He had never travelled in such comfort!

"You can access all the latest movies here," explained the woman, pointing to a massive plasma screen. "And this," she continued, as a machine sprang out of Zac's armrest, "is your personal popcorn popper."

The trip was ten hours, which wasn't long enough to enjoy everything on the blimp. First, Zac watched a movie. Then he had a foot massage and head rub. Then he discovered the in-seat virtual reality roller-coaster rides.

He was still riding *Iron Gutz*, the world's first virtual reality rollercoaster, when suddenly he felt a bump for real.

Zac checked the time on his SpyPad. It was 3:03 a.m. – nearly time to touch down. Perhaps the bump Zac felt was just the blimp coming in to land?

Then – **EURGH!**

The blimp lurched sideways, leaving Zac's stomach behind. *This is no ordinary landing!* Zac thought, worried.

He rushed to the window. Below, the lights of Hollywood lay spread out like Christmas lights. Mansions clung to the steep cliffs, a shimmering aqua swimming pool in every yard.

But none of it explained why the blimp was flying so crazily all of a sudden.

Inside the cabin, crystal bowls smashed on the floor, scattering chocolate bars everywhere. The lights flickered. *What's going on?* Zac hoped they weren't about to crash.

Zac scanned the skies for an answer. Then he saw it. A chopper was weaving in and out of the blimp's flight path!

What kind of idiot would fly so close to another aircraft? Zac thought furiously. The chopper's blades, whizzing so fast they were a blur, would slice through the blimp's outer lining in a flash!

Zac looked closely at the chopper. Inside the cabin sat a woman with blond hair piled high on her head. A hairless dog with bulging eyes and a diamond collar lay curled in her lap.

The woman waved her fist in Zac's direction. Zac noticed the sharp red nails, like claws, at the end of her fingers.

The woman looked an awful lot like Chrissie L'Estrange, the Hollywood actress. Everybody knew her — it was impossible not to. Chrissie and her little dog Poppet were on the cover of every magazine. Zac hated her movies.

Zac looked again. Now Chrissie was screaming something in his direction!

Zac was glad of his lip-reading training. He could understand her perfectly.

"GET OUTTA MY WAY, JERK!" she screeched. "DON'T YOU KNOW WHO I AM?" Her chopper swooped in front of the blimp.

Inside the blimp, Zac heard an announcement:

"This is your captain speaking. We apologize for this unexpected turbulence. The chopper will land on the helipad on top of the Hotel Deluxe. We will land there afterwards."

Zac thought he heard the captain mutter, "Even though we were here first."

A few minutes later, the blimp touched down on the helipad. Chrissie L'Estrange was already there, surrounded by fussing personal assistants.

I'll just go over there and clear things up, thought Zac to himself. But as soon as he took a step in Chrissie's direction, flashbulbs exploded in his eyes.

"Who are you? Are you Chrissie's latest boyfriend?" someone cried out of nowhere.

"What's your name? Who's your agent?"

Zac's mouth dropped open. *The paparazzi! Where did they come from?*

"He's no one," Zac heard one of them say. "Let's follow Chrissie."

And with that, the photographers and

reporters scattered from the helipad.

I'm not no one, Zac wanted to reply. *I'm a top spy here for a big premiere!*

Zac turned back to the blimp. But in the commotion, it had flown off without Zac noticing. Zac's backpack lay on the helipad. All of a sudden, he was alone in Hollywood – the strangest of all strange places.

CHAPTER... ...THREE

Zac's ears popped as the super-fast elevator swept him up to his penthouse on the fifty-first floor of the Hotel Deluxe. The doors opened directly into the suite, which was equipped with an ice cream machine and a wide-screen theatre.

Zac dumped his backpack on the king-sized bed. He clicked on the remote control and a giant TV screen dropped down from the ceiling.

An announcer with a stiff wave of blond hair was beaming at the camera.

"Stay tuned for a Channel One exclusive report into spying in the modern age," she was saying. "We reveal how spy agencies are looking for ways to make their investigations quicker and more efficient."

Leon would probably watch that, the big nerd, thought Zac, smiling to himself.

THUD! THUD! THUD!

Someone was knocking at the door of his suite – loudly!

"Room service!" called a voice.

Zac got up and opened the door.

"Hot dog?" said the pimply guy standing in Zac's doorway. He held out a tray of hot dogs zig-zagged with yellow mustard.

"Er, I didn't order a hot dog," said Zac.

"Take one. They're delicious!" said the guy, and then he leaned in closer.

"I'm a GIB agent," he muttered. "We tracked your arrival in the blimp. We've actually been trying to get in touch with you since yesterday, but it seems the lining of the blimp interfered with your SpyPad receptor and blocked all incoming messages.

"No one at GIB knows why you're in town," he added, "but you've got a new mission. Now take the hot dog."

He handed Zac a hot dog and left, singing, "Have a nice day!" as he went.

Zac stared after him, feeling confused. Why didn't GIB know why Zac was in Hollywood? After all, it was GIB who invited him to the *Covert Operations* premiere! And if they didn't, who did?

I guess I'd better find out what my mission is, thought Zac as he checked out the hot dog. There was a sticker on the bun, so tiny he had to squint to read it. It said "FTP enabled."

The mission must be a file inside the hot dog! But there was a problem. How was Zac going to upload a mission into his SpyPad from a *hot dog*?

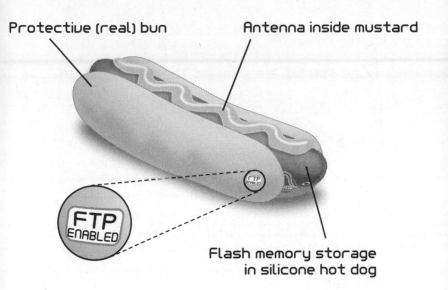

Protective (real) bun

Antenna inside mustard

FTP ENABLED

Flash memory storage in silicone hot dog

Without smearing mustard on the casing, Zac held the hot dog up to his SpyPad. A green light flickered on. His SpyPad was Bluetooth compatible...and so was the hot dog. The mission was uploading wirelessly!

CLASSIFIED
FOR THE EYES OF ZAC POWER ONLY

MESSAGE RECEIVED
SATURDAY 4:54 A.M.

Cinemania, a Hollywood film studio, is spending millions on a mysterious invention called ThoughtVision.

In fact, they're spending more than they do on producing films. This may be innocent, but GIB is suspicious.

YOUR MISSION

• Work out what ThoughtVision does and locate a prototype for GIB.

MISSION TIME REMAINING
12 HOURS 6 MINUTES

END

MUSTARD MODE
>>> OFF

So now Zac had two missions. To solve the ThoughtVision mystery and to figure out who'd invited him to the premiere. But the premiere was only twelve hours away!

Before leaving the penthouse suite, Zac paused in front of the mirror to slick some product into his hair. There was no way he wanted to look scruffy on the stylish streets of Hollywood!

Zac supposed that the obvious place to start the ThoughtVision investigation was at the Cinemania Studios. But before he could hail a taxi, a vehicle pulled up right in front of him.

The passenger door opened and a voice wafted out. "Please, come inside."

Zac had to step back to take in the full size of the car. It was a yellow stretch Hummer. Its engine rumbled loudly.

Zac climbed in. But no one was driving the car! The voice, which was obviously computerized, said, "Welcome to AutoJeeves, the driverless chauffeur service. Where would you like to go?"

"Cinemania Studios," replied Zac.

Ah, the Hollywood lifestyle, thought Zac, as the stretch Hummer took off into the honking traffic.

The Hummer pulled up outside the fancy iron gates of Cinemania. Through the fence, Zac could see row after row of sets from old movies. There were people everywhere, zipping around the huge studio lot in white golf carts, or sitting around in canvas chairs with their names on the back. The studio must keep shooting movies all night!

A security guard stood at the gates, where a line of people waited to get in.

"Yes? What is your business here?" asked the guard mechanically. "I have a script meeting with Mr. Spielford," Zac heard someone say. "I am Chrissie L'Estrange's plastic surgeon," said a woman just in front of Zac.

"You?" the guard asked Zac.

A big part of spying was pretending to be someone you weren't. But Zac was totally exhausted. It had been a long night. For once, he struggled to think of a false identity. "I've got an appointment with Poppet L'Estrange," blurted Zac at last. "I'm...I'm...I'm her hair stylist."

The guard eyeballed Zac silently.

I'm such an idiot! Zac panicked. *Who'd believe a hairless dog has its own hairdresser?*

Zac's spirits plummeted. No way would he get past the security guard and into Cinemania now!

Was the unthinkable about to happen? Was Zac Power actually going to fail a mission?

CHAPTER... ...FOUR

"Poppet L'Estrange?" repeated the guard.

"Er, yes," said Zac, uncertainly.

"What time is your appointment?"

Zac checked his watch. It was 5:37 a.m.

MISSION
TIME LEFT 11 : 22 : 08
GIB HRS MINS SECS
05:37:52 AM
FRI

"Six o'clock," Zac said, sounding more confident than he felt.

"It's that trailer over there," said the guard finally, opening the gates. The guard shook his head in pity. "You're Poppet's fourth stylist this month," he added.

I guess nothing's too weird for Hollywood, Zac thought.

Zac headed in the direction of Poppet L'Entrange's trailer to avoid suspicion. All the stars (and their dogs) had their own luxury trailers to sit in between filming scenes. The more famous the star, the bigger the trailer.

That must be someone really important, Zac thought as he passed a silver trailer the size

of two buses, complete with a satellite dish on top. There was a name on the door in a star-shaped tag that said "Caroline."

I wonder who that is? thought Zac.

Then Zac noticed a golf cart puttering to a stop nearby. A woman got out, yakking into her cellphone.

"We aim to supply each unit with a

camera by next year," she said. "It will cost a lot at first, but think of the savings later on."

The woman was so wrapped up in her conversation, she left the keys in the golf cart's ignition as she walked off.

Seizing his chance, Zac jumped into the golf cart and sped off. Now he could search Cinemania properly!

Zac was flying over a speed bump when the golf cart's radio crackled to life.

"Attention all security units. A golf cart has been stolen. Suspect has cool hair, repeat cool hair. Likely identity: Zachary Power."

Ah-ha! Cinemania was definitely not a genuine movie studio! Otherwise, how would they know his name?

Suddenly, Zac heard a weird crunching sound behind him. There, not ten metres away, was a security guard in a golf cart, cracking his knuckles!

The guard's neck was as thick as a utility pole. He looked more machine than human. And he was heading in Zac's direction – FAST!

Zac slammed his foot on the accelerator. His cart shot forward, but not fast enough. The guard was closing in!

Zac sped toward what looked like the Wild Wild West. It was an old film set, cluttered with horse troughs and abandoned mine shafts.

Desperately, he wove between the

obstacles. This was harder than *Mario Kart*! And if he crashed, Zac knew he couldn't just start all over again.

Zac slammed into a barrel and sent it flying. The cart flipped. Zac flew out and...

KER-RUNCH!

He landed flat on his face. The barrel slammed into the guard's cart, knocking him over like a bowling pin.

Zac jumped up and ran for it.

Gotta hide, he thought. His face stung from where he'd landed on the gravel.

Up ahead, Zac saw a haunted house set from a horror movie. The windows were boarded up, the door nailed shut.

Perfect...if I can figure out how to get in.

Frantically, Zac rattled every board on every window.

RIIIIIP!

A board came loose and Zac wriggled through the window. Velvety darkness swallowed him up instantly.

Blindly, he felt his way farther inside the house. All of a sudden, Zac went cold. *What was that sound?*

Footsteps!

"Zac Power!" thundered a voice.

The room flooded with yellow light. Zac's eyes throbbed. He'd been caught!

Standing in front of him was the guard from before! Hang on...hadn't Zac left him behind outside?

Wait…thought Zac. *What's that weird lump on his neck?*

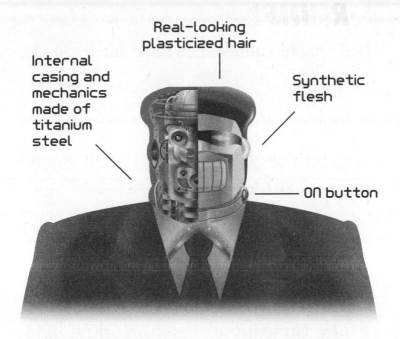

Real-looking
plasticized hair

Internal
casing and
mechanics
made of
titanium
steel

Synthetic
flesh

ON button

An ON button! No wonder this guard looked like the one from the cart. *And like the one at the front gate,* Zac realized.

The guards were all androids!

A new GIB ruling required all spies to wear PitStink capsules under their arms in case of android attack. When broken, the capsule releases a vile stink from the armpit.

As hard as he could, Zac pumped his right arm up and down three times until he felt a blast of gas.

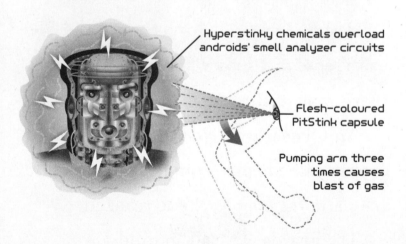

Hyperstinky chemicals overload androids' smell analyzer circuits

Flesh-coloured PitStink capsule

Pumping arm three times causes blast of gas

"Halt, Zac Power," boomed the android, lumbering toward him.

Zac lifted his right arm. Powerful stink waves wafted out — a cross between rotting meat and a wet dog.

"Halt, Zac Pow— errrrgh!" screeched the android. It dropped to the floor, holding its nose. Smoke curled from its ears. The PitStink had short-circuited its wiring!

Hastily, Zac stepped over the android. He had a sense that somewhere in this building there was a clue about ThoughtVision. *Why else would it be guarded so closely?* Zac thought. *And by fierce, ruthless androids?*

CHAPTER... ...FIVE

In one corner, Zac spotted an old staircase.

Could lead to an attic, Zac thought, placing a sneaker on the first step. *That's the perfect place to hide information about ThoughtVision.*

Suddenly —

Ffffffffftftftftftftftft!

A bunch of bats appeared from nowhere and flew straight at Zac's face!

Zac's heart pounded, but he pushed

the bats aside and reminded himself that he was in a haunted house. The bats were on strings. They were made of rubber!

Just part of the film set, Zac remembered, breathing quickly.

He kept climbing the stairs. At the top was a very small door. Zac firmly pushed it open.

What lay behind was no dusty old attic! Instead, there were rows and rows of high-tech laptops. Zac's spy senses tingled. He was onto something!

Zac raced to the nearest computer and selected Display Recent Documents. There it was — ThoughtVision_Blueprints.doc!

Zac double-clicked. The screen filled with diagrams. On the left, Zac saw a picture of a movie camera. A bunch of wavy lines labelled "Thought Waves" wiggled toward it. Labels and arrows pointed in all directions.

Zac's brain hurt trying to understand it all. He needed Leon's help. He plugged his SpyPad into the laptop, uploaded the diagrams, then punched in Leon's number.

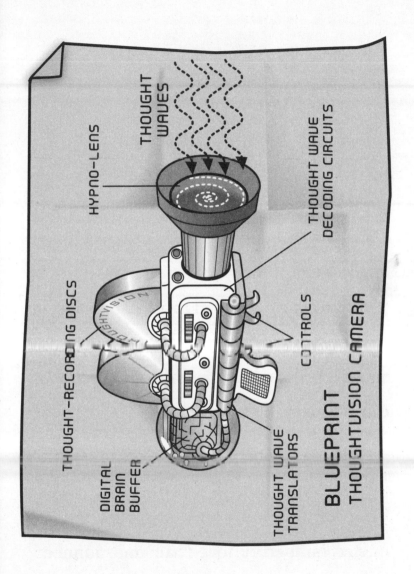

THOUGHT WAVES

HYPNO-LENS

THOUGHT WAVE
DECODING CIRCUITS

THOUGHT-RECORDING DISCS

CONTROLS

DIGITAL
BRAIN
BUFFER

THOUGHT WAVE
TRANSLATORS

BLUEPRINT
THOUGHTVISION CAMERA

He glanced at his watch. 7:47 a.m. –
Leon would be up by now. But when Zac
tried to call, there was no signal!

Gotta get outside, Zac thought. He ran in
the direction of the stairs, but then changed
his mind. *The android might have rebooted his
system by now*, he thought.

During his GIB Spy Academy training,
Zac had learned loads of tricky escapes.
Now was the time to try one out!

Zac jumped onto a chair and punched

out a skylight overhead. He was going to attempt a Multi-Storey Roof Jump, an escape reserved for the bravest of spies.

Zac wriggled through the skylight and onto the roof. As he looked over the edge, he heard a noise on the staircase inside. The android was back! *Good thing I didn't take the stairs*, Zac thought.

If he took a big run-up and timed it perfectly...yes, he probably could jump off the building and land on the roof of the moving golf cart below. No android guard would think of looking for him there!

The golf cart was in the perfect position. It was now or never!

He sped toward the edge of the building.

He took a deep breath and... JUMPED!

He was in free fall...and then...

THUNK!

Zac landed squarely on the cart's roof. "What was that?" came a girl's voice from inside the cart.

Zac froze. He *knew* that voice...

An image flashed into his mind of the enormous silver trailer that he'd seen earlier. He remembered the name

"Caroline" written on the door…

Caz is short for Caroline! Zac realized with a shock.

Caz was an enemy spy for the enemy organization BIG. And if Caz was here at Cinemania, that meant the two were somehow linked. *But how?*

Zac was racking his brains when he  felt a text message come through on his SpyPad. Lucky he'd set it to vibrate mode!

Have you heard the news? BIG's profits down 50%. Ha Ha Ha

>>> SIGNED: Leon

MESSAGE DELIVERY
>>> VIBRATE

Now wasn't the time for spy industry gossip! Zac needed proper help from Leon, like an online search to work out how BIG and Cinemania were related.

But I can't call Leon from here! Caz will hear every word! thought Zac.

There was only one thing to do.

He flung himself sideways, rolling off the cart and landing heavily in the gutter with a muffled "urgh!"

Just as he had planned, the cart kept on driving. He didn't think anyone had seen him jump off.

Right, now to call Leon, Zac thought, dusting off his T-shirt and digging out his SpyPad.

Then he heard a booming voice. "There you are!"

Oh no, the android guards! Zac panicked.

"You're needed on set, Grave," continued the voice, which belonged to a beefy man wearing a "Film Crew" T-shirt. His name was stitched on the back – Brutus.

Brutus grabbed Zac's arm. There was no getting away. Brutus gripped like an angry pit bull.

"You're ready for your big stunt scene, right?" said Brutus.

CHAPTER... ...SIX

Stunt scene? Zac's brain whirred.

There was a child star called Dave "Grave" Danger – the most extreme stuntman ever. He was twelve, Zac's age. Brutus must have seen Zac's commando roll and mistaken him for Grave!

"In here," said Brutus, steering Zac into a film studio as big as an aircraft hanger. On the door, a sign read:

Zac looked around. The studio was crawling with people wheeling cameras and shouting into megaphones. Right away, someone rushed toward Zac and fluffed his hair. His nose was dabbed with makeup.

The makeup part was weird. Zac had hated it when enemy agents had given him

a makeover as revenge, and he sure didn't like it now! *Still*, he thought, *it's nice to be treated like a star for once.*

"OK, Grave," said Brutus, checking a clipboard. "First up is the scene where you run through a glass window."

Zac nodded. *No worries! Bet they pre-shatter the glass so it only* looks *like you're breaking it*, he thought.

"Then," continued Brutus, "you'll wrestle Bessie."

The entire set went silent as Brutus led Bessie in on a massive silver chain. Bessie was a wild black bear!

In a lame attempt to make her look friendly, someone had tied a pink bow around Bessie's neck. It didn't work. Bessie's lips were peeled back in a snarl, giving Zac a perfect view of her big, white fangs dripping with gloopy spit. Great.

Spy school didn't cover wrestling black bears. *But if Dave "Grave" Danger can do it, so can I,* figured Zac.

He quickly glanced at his watch and grimaced. It was already 8:31a.m.!

Zac desperately needed to keep going with the mission. But if he told the crew he wasn't Dave "Grave" Danger, they'd call security. And Zac didn't want to mess with those androids again.

Then he had an idea. He let out a high-pitched scream.

"Where is the lemon-flavoured orange drink and brownies I asked for? I cannot work under these conditions!" He tossed his head and pouted. "I WANT to go back to my dressing room RIGHT NOW."

Zac was putting on his best impression of a celebrity tantrum.

And when I'm back in Grave's dressing room, I'll sneak off, Zac thought.

The crew just stood and watched Zac's tantrum. No one seemed surprised.

"OK, Grave," said Brutus. "I get it. You're too scared to wrestle Bessie."

Too scared? *I'm not too scared,* Zac huffed to himself. *I'm just too busy!* But he couldn't go back to the dressing room now. The next quickest way out was to just wrestle Bessie and then make a run for it.

"Forget the brownies," said Zac sulkily.

Brutus lead Zac over to a thick piece of glass. On the other side, he could just make out the blurry shape of Bessie standing on her hind legs, flexing her claws.

"Quiet, please," called a voice. "Roll camera – and – ACTION!"

CHAPTER... ...SEVEN

CRACK!

Zac smashed into the glass window at top speed. Glass showered down around him.

Cool! he thought. *Now to wrestle Bess—*

WHUMP! Bessie landed heavily on Zac's back, growling dangerously. It was like being hugged by an especially loving aunt – who's hairy and stinks of salmon.

Suddenly Zac remembered something his grandma had told him.

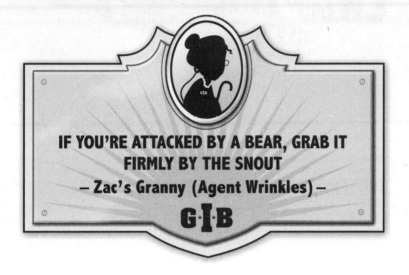

IF YOU'RE ATTACKED BY A BEAR, GRAB IT FIRMLY BY THE SNOUT
— Zac's Granny (Agent Wrinkles) —

Or was that alligators? wondered Zac. His grandma tended to talk a lot.

Either way, now was the time to try out her advice!

Zac grabbed Bessie's slobbery muzzle. The enormous bear gave a "humph?"

of surprise. Then she let go of Zac! She rubbed her snout and looked hurt.

"CUT!" yelled the director. "Not bad, Grave. But you need to look…braver. Let's do it again."

Zac shrugged. Surely it wouldn't be long until he could sneak away…

"ACTION!" bellowed the director.

Zac ran toward a second sheet of glass. But before he got there, the director yelled out, "CUT!"

What now? thought Zac, frustrated.

"There's a hair on the camera lens. Let's go again."

Now Zac could understand why it sometimes took a whole year to make a movie! After every take, a new sheet of glass had to be brought in. Bessie's fur was brushed and Zac's makeup touched up.

Precious time slipped away. 9:12 a.m. 10:43 a.m. Soon it was midday!

"OK, let's break for lunch," called the director at last.

"I'll be in my trailer!" Zac answered, disappearing into the shadows.

The back of the studio was a jumble of camera equipment, lights and dusty old sets.

Anything could be hidden back here, thought Zac. *Hey — what's that?*

Zac noticed a door, bolted shut. A sign read, "Camera Tests."

Something clicked in Zac's mind. Those blueprints said ThoughtVision was some kind of camera.

This might get the mission back on track, thought Zac.

Zac grabbed the SpyPad from his pocket and flipped it over. He slid the back casing off and pulled out a skeleton key. It was a special GIB-issue key that could open any lock in the world.

Zac jiggled the key in the lock. It was stiff, but it opened. He inched the huge metal door open. Pressing close to the walls, he snuck into the room.

A man sat on a chair facing away from Zac. He was looking into a movie camera. Zac couldn't quite make out who was behind the camera.

"You can trust me," the man sitting in the chair said. He sounded like he was about to cry.

Then Zac noticed a screen above the man's head. As soon as the man said anything, the screen displayed different words above his head.

"I would never betray BIG," the man stammered. But the screen said:

I HATE BIG.

"I know what you're *really* thinking!" said a girl from behind the camera.

It sounded like Caz. And she was obviously using a ThoughtVision camera.

What evil technology! A camera that read thoughts as it filmed. But why would BIG want a camera like that?

Suddenly, the pieces dropped into place in Zac's mind. BIG's profits were down. And that news report, back in the hotel, had said spies needed quicker ways to work!

Questioning people with a camera that read minds would be *the* quickest possible way to find out all sorts of secrets. It would be way more reliable than any truth serum or special investigations.

A movie studio would be the perfect front for an operation like ThoughtVision. BIG probably invented Cinemania to cover its tracks.

That explained why the films Cinemania made were so terrible. A movie like *Short Fuse*, where a kid wrestled a bear, would be box office poison!

"Soon we'll have people working these cameras full-time," Caz crowed. "We can't afford to waste our own good people on boring work like that."

"I see," said the man in the chair. But the screen displayed his true thoughts:

I HATE YOU!

"We're going to brainwash enemy spies, including that loser Zac Power," said Caz, starting to giggle. "Zac Power's going to work for BIG!"

CHAPTER... EIGHT

At that moment, all Zac wanted in the world was to yank Caz's bushy pigtails.

How would BIG try to brainwash him? And more importantly, how dare Caz call him a loser?

He was furious, but he took some deep breaths. *Stay calm,* he told himself, *she's about to spill the beans on her evil plan.*

"Using Cinemania Studios as our front, we've shot a new spy movie, *Covert Operations*," said Caz, sounding thrilled with herself. "It's *packed* with subliminal messages."

Subliminal messages? thought Zac. He knew they were words or pictures in a film that flashed up too fast for you to notice. Subliminal messages could convince you to do things against your will. *Things like working for BIG!*

Suddenly, he heard something. *Beep! Beep!* It was getting louder.

Annoyed, Caz looked up from the ThoughtVision camera. "What is it, G5-382?" she snapped.

There was the clank of metal. Zac peered out from behind a stack of boxes.

Another android security guard!

"Heat sensors engaged," said the android in its dull, robotic voice.

"What?" asked Caz, irritably.

"Human heat detected in northeast quadrant of the room," droned the android.

Oh no! Zac was busted!

The ThoughtVision camera was so close and bringing back that prototype *was* an essential part of his mission! But if Zac didn't scram right that very second, Caz and BIG would get him for sure.

I'll have to capture the camera some other way, Zac thought grimly.

He scanned the room for ways to escape. But Caz had blocked one door, and the android was guarding the other!

There was an air vent high up on the wall. Zac lunged onto a wobbly stack of packing crates. He leapt at a pipe running along the ceiling. Then, swinging like a monkey along the pipe, he kicked in the air vent.

Now to wriggle through the hole...

"It's Zac Power!" Caz squealed. "You androids are supposed to be saving us money. Now show me you're worth it! Get him!"

It was a squeeze, but Zac was just small enough to slip through the vent. There was no way the massive metal android could follow him!

Zac popped out the other side, Caz's furious screams ringing in his ears.

Zac spotted a brand new black Harley Davidson parked nearby. He grabbed his GIB skeleton key and started the ignition. The Harley rumbled to life.

Zac's SpyPad bleeped an alarm.

It was 1:33 p.m. Zac still had time to stop the premiere and capture the ThoughtVision camera. Zac realized Caz would be at the premiere, and she could lead him to the prototype.

Zac tapped "Nightshade Theatre" into his SpyPad's GPS system and roared out of the studio lot.

His mind was racing as fast as the bike. There'd probably be a red carpet at the premiere, and paparazzi taking photos.

Zac checked his outfit. Skate shoes, sweaty T-shirt, dirty jeans. His hair product had long since melted away.

He couldn't turn up to a red carpet event looking like that. A spy has standards!

CHAPTER... ...NINE

Zac needed a cool new suit. Not too formal, maybe a scruffy jacket and skinny pants, like rock stars wear.

But where would I get something like that? Zac wondered.

"Turn left here for the Hollywood Walk of Fame," said the computerized voice of the SpyPad in his pocket. "Shopping mall and the Nightshade Theatre."

Just what Zac needed!

With a screech of tires, Zac took a sharp left onto the Hollywood Walk of Fame. He pulled up outside a shop called Leroy's Outfitters to the Stars.

The shop was packed with amazing clothes. One wall was full of T-shirts, another of motorcycle boots. He'd never seen so much cool stuff in one place before. He just couldn't leave without trying a few things on. Surely he had time…

A few outfits later, the sound of the radio snapped him back to reality.

"Another sunny day in Hollywood. The time is 3:00 p.m."

Zac raced out of the shop with his new

suit on. He'd wasted too much time! He had to get to the Nightshade Theatre.

Zac was concentrating so hard, he didn't notice a shadowy figure behind him —

Ugh!

Someone shoved him in the back!

Zac tumbled forward, his hands out in front of him to break his fall.

But it wasn't hard concrete he felt as he fell. It was something squishy.

WET CEMENT!

Zac was on the Hollywood Walk of Fame, where stars left their handprints in the cement. And someone had replaced the ordinary sidewalk with the quick-drying kind. Zac was stuck fast!

He looked around for help, but everyone was busily rushing into shops. Joggers wearing sweatbands jumped over him and glamorous mothers pushing strollers swerved around him.

Time raced on. 3:17 p.m. 4:06 p.m. 4:45 p.m.! But Zac wasn't going anywhere.

Until he remembered something.

Leon made him keep a DynaWrite pen in his pocket at all times. "You might need it to do Sudoku puzzles," he'd said. "The explosive device hidden inside could be useful, too."

If Zac could detonate the DynaWrite pen, he could explode the cement around his hands and escape.

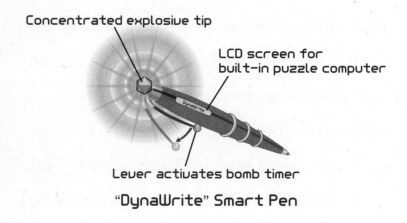

Concentrated explosive tip

LCD screen for built-in puzzle computer

Lever activates bomb timer

"DynaWrite" Smart Pen

But how am I going to get the pen out of my pocket when my hands are stuck? Zac wondered.

Zac was no gymnast, but his spy training had kept him strong and flexible. If he could get upside down, the DynaWrite pen might drop out of his pocket.

He launched himself skyward. Kicking his legs wildly, he held the handstand. But the explosive pen stayed in his pocket!

Zac wiggled his body. He felt the pen moving. He wiggled a bit more.

At last! The DynaWrite pen fell out onto the cement.

Now, to detonate! thought Zac, kicking his legs down.

He didn't know the rules on detonating an explosive device with your nose. Perhaps there weren't any?

Hardly daring to breathe, Zac tapped the red button on the end of the pen with the tip of his nose. He leaned back as —

BOOOOM!

His hands were free! And his nose was still attached to his face!

He checked the time on his watch.

Zac was too late. *Covert Operations* had already begun!

CHAPTER... ...TEN

The movie had started, but Zac wasn't quitting. Showering concrete dust every-where, he ran down the Hollywood Walk of Fame toward the Nightshade Theatre.

Zac knew he had to get inside the theatre to stop innocent spies from being brainwashed. But if he saw a single second of the film, he could be brainwashed himself!

I need protection, he thought. Thinking quickly, he pulled on his sunglasses. Then he stuffed his iPod earphones in, turning the music up loud. *BIG could have planted subliminal messages in the soundtrack, too,* he figured.

Zac ran up the red carpet. Paparazzi were everywhere.

"Look!" someone yelled. "It's Poppet L'Estrange's stylist!"

"Great suit!" called a TV interviewer, as Zac raced past and into the theatre.

His throat was dry. Passing the candy counter, he grabbed a bucket-sized soft drink.

Zac burst into the theatre. The audience

was packed with spies. Some he recognized from GIB!

He avoided looking at the screen. Zac scanned the walls for the projector. He had to stop the screening!

But how? In his mind Zac ran through his gadgets.

Electronic snake-charmer? No good.

Edible dictionary? No way.

How about my trusty slingshot?

Zac felt in his pockets for ammo, but they were empty. Everything must have fallen out when he did the handstand back on the Hollywood Walk of Fame.

What else in a theatre was small and round? ChocBalls!

That'll do! thought Zac, snatching a box from a dazed spy sitting nearby. Zac whipped round to the back of the theatre. High up on the wall was the projector, safe behind thick glass. *But the ChocBalls feel too light!* If he wanted to smash the projector, Zac calculated that he'd have to hit it in exactly the same place ten times in a row. That would take superior shooting!

He loaded his slingshot with the first ChocBall, and snapped the rubber band.

It whizzed through the air — and hit the glass dead centre. Zac reloaded with a second ChocBall.

THUNK!

The second ChocBall made contact.

"What's that noise?" asked an usher angrily. He looked familiar to Zac...

The usher was another android! In fact, Zac suddenly realized, *all* the ushers in the theatre were androids.

Desperately, Zac fired more ChocBalls at the projector.

Seven – eight – nine –

Android ushers appeared from every direction. They were closing in on Zac.

Zac loaded his tenth ChocBall. He took aim, screwing one eye shut for a better view.

But as Zac prepared to fire, an android usher ran up behind him. Its robotic arm reached out toward Zac's neck just as he fired the tenth ball.

SNAP!

It shattered the glass and the projector behind it in a shower of sparks. The movie screen blanked out.

The audience erupted. Spies jumped out of their seats. Android ushers tried to stop anyone leaving. A girl who sounded very much like Caz screamed, "Nooooooo!"

Zac spun round. An android was almost on top of him! Lightning fast, Zac tipped the entire bucket-sized soft drink over its head. Instantly, the acids and sugars in the drink ate through the android's synthetic skin. The android dropped to the floor, one eyeball hanging out on a single piece of red wire.

I really should stay away from soft drinks, thought Zac, as the android shuddered and sparked.

Then a blurry figure raced past Zac. Bushy pigtails, a camera bag over her shoulder — Caz! *And she's probably carrying the Thought Vision prototype!*

Zac took off after Caz and the prototype. But Caz, sneaky as ever, handed the camera bag to an android usher and ran off.

Should I capture Caz, or stay and secure the prototype? Zac wondered.

He hated Caz more than boy bands and Homework Club. But his mission was to bring back the prototype!

He sighed. Caz streaked away as Zac turned to the android.

"You know, I've heard there's a top agent here looking for androids to star in a new movie," said Zac slyly.

"Really?" said the android, loosening its grip on the camera bag. "Where?"

"Oh, somewhere over there," said Zac vaguely, pointing across to the other side of the theatre.

The android spun around for a better

look. Zac slipped the camera bag from its arm and ran.

The Harley was still parked where Zac had left it, outside the theatre. He roared off, slinging the camera bag over his shoulder. He called Leon and put him on speaker.

"Leon! Can you get me out of here?" he yelled over the Harley's growl. "I've got the prototype!"

"I'll plot your co-ordinates on GIB's central mission computer," said Leon.

Zac heard a crash as a bunch of android ushers burst out of the Nightshade Theatre and started chasing him down the street.

"Will it take long?" yelled Zac.

"Nope," Leon said. "There's a GIB rescue chopper in your area. Ride to the Hollywood sign on top of the hill, climb up and we'll grab you from there."

"Got it," said Zac, speeding off.

The Hollywood sign loomed in front of him. He leapt off the Harley and raced to the bottom of the enormous letter "H." It was a least four storeys high and made of flat sheets of steel.

It would be really difficult to climb. Difficult that is, if Zac's shoes hadn't been specially modified for situations like this.

He flipped the Octopod Mode switch on the tongue of his left shoe. At once, powerful suckers sprung out of the soles. Zac stepped onto the letter "H" and started walking up.

He was almost at the top when he heard voices below — he was being followed!

"Hey, Grave! You're needed for another stunt!" called Brutus.

"You told me there was an agent looking for androids!" snarled the android usher.

"What's your plan for Poppet L'Estrange's next look?" called a reporter.

But the whirring chopper blades drowned them out. The chopper door opened and the GIB rescue team threw a rope down to Zac. He grabbed hold of it and was instantly hauled upward to safety.

As soon as he sat down inside the chopper, Zac's SpyPad rang. It was a call from Agent Bum Smack – Zac's mum.

"I hear GIB invited you to a premiere,"

said his mum. "Lucky thing! You'd better write a thank you note to GIB as soon as you get home."

"Sure, mum," said Zac. He could fill her in on what *really* happened later on.

"Did you enjoy the movie?" his mum asked.

"Yeah, I really got into it," said Zac, laughing. "Especially the stunt scenes."

Your mission: read all the books
in the Zac Power series ...

POISON ISLAND   DEEP WATERS   FROZEN FEAR   MIND GAMES

NIGHT RAID   TOMB OF DOOM   LUNAR STRIKE   SUDDEN DROP

END